MW00763445

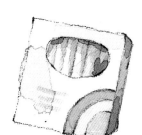

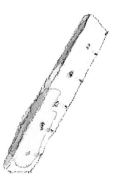
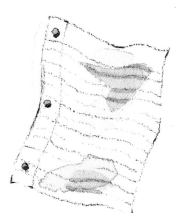

Daddy's
Back-to-School
Shopping
Adventure

by Alan Lawrence Sitomer

Illustrated by Abby Carter

DISNEP • HYPERION

Los Angeles   New York

Text copyright © 2015 by Alan Lawrence Sitomer
Illustrations copyright © 2015 by Abby Carter

All rights reserved. Published by Disney • Hyperion, an imprint of Disney Book Group. No part of this book may
be reproduced or transmitted in any form or by any means, electronic or mechanical, including photocopying,
recording, or by any information storage and retrieval system, without written permission from the publisher.
For information address Disney • Hyperion, 125 West End Avenue, New York, New York 10023.

Printed in Malaysia
First Edition, June 2015
1 3 5 7 9 10 8 6 4 2
H106-9333-5-15060

Library of Congress Cataloging-in-Publication Data

Sitomer, Alan Lawrence.
Daddy and the back-to-school shopping adventure / written by Alan Lawrence
Sitomer ; illustrated by Abby Carter.—First edition.
pages cm
Summary: When Mommy and Daddy take Jake and Jenny back-to-school
shopping, they are determined to stick to their list but when Mommy steps
away, requests for items not on the list abound, including one from Daddy.
ISBN 978-1-4231-8421-8
[1. Shopping—Fiction. 2. Father and child—Fiction. 3. Humorous
stories.] I. Carter, Abby, illustrator. II. Title.
PZ7.S6228Dae 2015
[E]—dc23   2013044767

Reinforced binding
Visit www.DisneyBooks.com

Dedicated to
Quinny Bear and the Goose

"Get ready to put
some pep in your step,
my little Pickle Quackers.
Today we're going
back-to-school shopping.

"And what's the number-one rule
for school-supply shopping?"

"We only buy what's on the list,"
Jenny and Jake replied at the same time.

"Exxxxx-actly,"
Daddy said.

"Why do parents always say things a hundred million times?" Jake asked Jenny.

"It's so they don't grow kangaroo tails."

"Oh," Jake said, nodding his head.
"That makes sense."

"Pencils?"
"Check."

"Erasers?"
"Check."

"Notebook paper?"
"Check."

"Daddy, can I have this?" Jake said.

"Oh, Daddy," Jenny said, "can we buy that?"

Daddy rolled his eyes.
"Hello? We have a list,"
he answered.

"I'll tell you what we **can** do, my little Pickle Quackers. . . . We can invent a new back-to-school clothing style."

"Oh, Mommy,"
said Jake.

"Look at us,"
Jenny called out.

"Very fashionable.
Squeeze together.
I want a picture,"
Mommy said.

"Can I get a trampoline?"

"I want a pogo stick!"

"And a portable popcorn maker!"

"I only have one thing to say,"
Daddy answered.
"Is it on the list?"

"Honey, I'm gonna go pick up a few small things for the house while we're here," Mommy said. "Meet ya in a few."

"Take your time, dear.

I got this."

"I want a stuffed penguin."

"I want a choo-choo train."

"I want a monkey."

Jake turned to Jenny.
"They sell monkeys here?"

"No," she answered.
"But we could stop for one
on the way home."

"Great idea!"
Jake said.

"Daddy, we want a
monkey!!"

"You got it!" Daddy answered. "As long as it's on the . . .

Oh my goodness."

"My old lunch box!

I used to have this exact same
one when I was a kid,"
Daddy said.
"I have to buy it."

"Uh, Daddy . . ." Jake said.

Jenny crossed her arms.

"Is it on the list?"

"you don't understand," Daddy said. "When I was a boy, this was my favorite, favorite thing in the whole wide world."

"But is it on the list?"

"Guys, you're not quite getting it," Daddy reasoned. "See, there's this thing called **nostalgia**. It's when you get a warm feeling about something from your past that . . ."

"Not seeing it here."

"Hmmm. Okay.
I'll make you a deal,"
said Daddy.

"Glow-in-the-dark
glue sticks!"

"Orange and
pink glitter tape
dispensers!"

"Strawberry-scented
pencil boxes!"

"Sparkly purple
wet wipes!"

"Electronic
garbage-truck
pencil sharpener!"

"Neon
paper clips!"

"Gulp."

"I guess I'll just put this back.
Meet you at the checkout,"
said Daddy sadly.

"PSst! Mommy! Jake and I have a great idea," Jenny whispered.

"**Oh, Daddy. . .**"
said Jenny.

"Even though you didn't get us
a monkey . . ."

"And we really wanted a monkey,"
Jake added,

"We got you a present."

"You did?"

"The LUNCH BOX!"

"You little sneaks. Come here right now!
I need to do some Pickle Quacker tickling!"

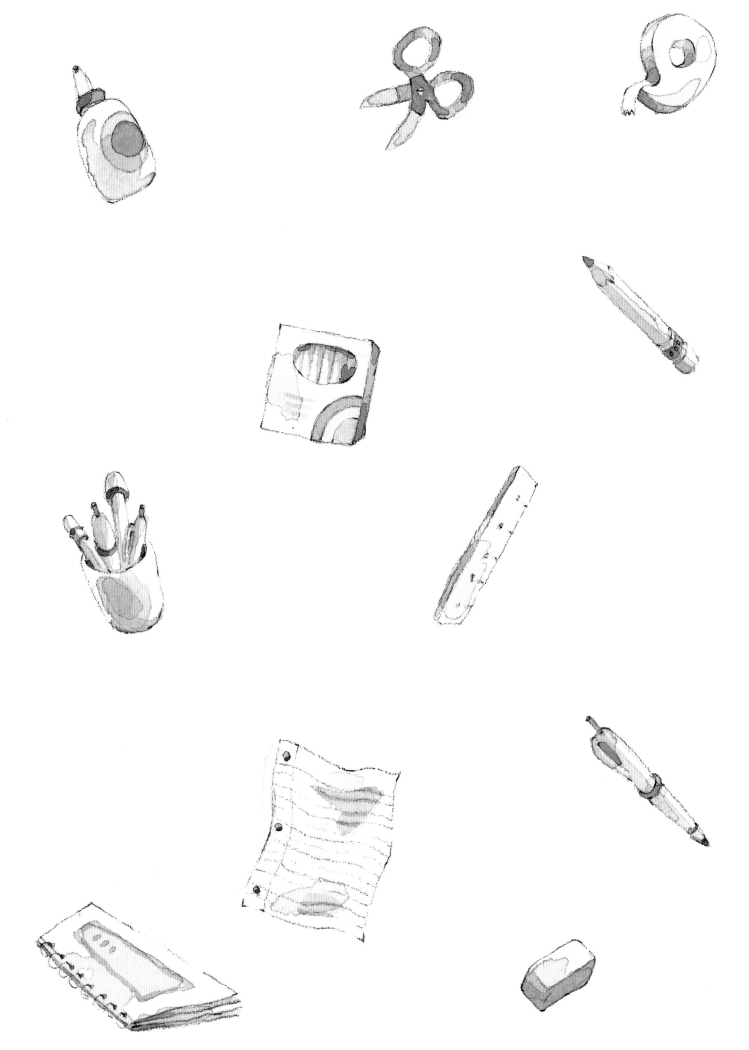

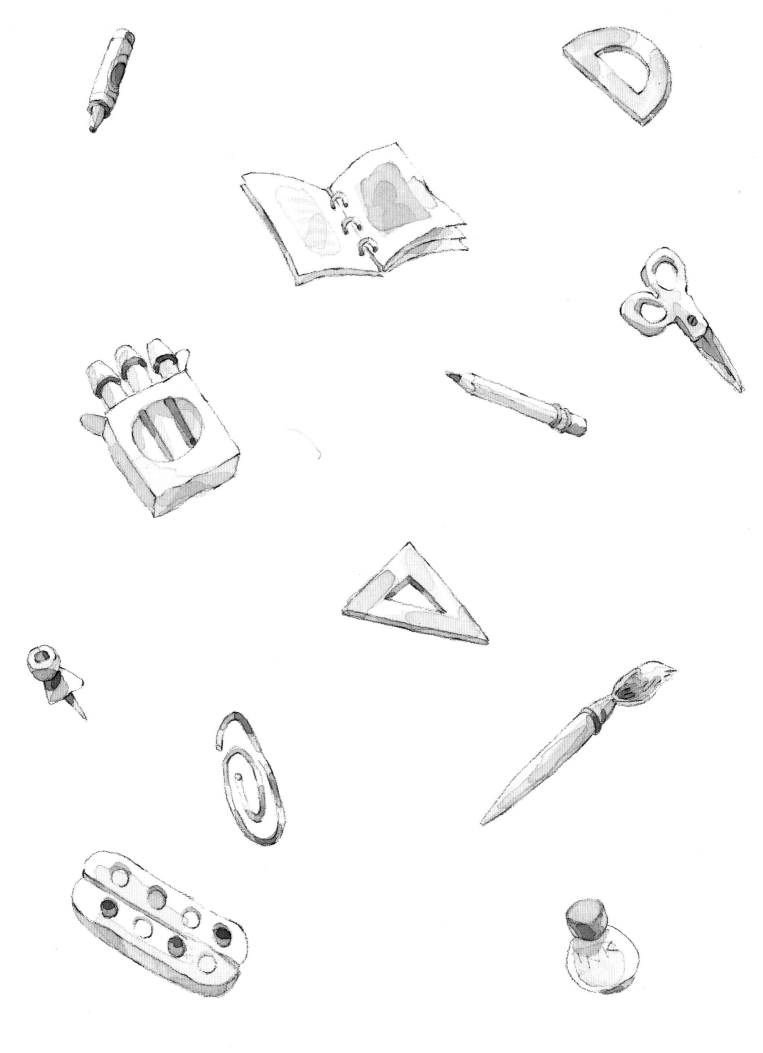